SURPRISE, STEGOSAURUS!

based on text by Dawn Bentley

Illustrated by Karen Carr

For Alexander. Love, Aunt Dawn. — D.B.

*Dedicated with love to my sister-in-law, Laura J. M. Gauer, with plans for
better days ahead. — K.C.*

Published by Soundprints Division of Trudy Corporation, Norwalk, Connecticut.

Book design: Marcin Pilchowski
Editor: Laura Gates Galvin
Editorial assistance: Brian E. Giblin

First Edition 2004
10 9 8 7 6 5 4 3 2 1
Printed in China

Acknowledgements:
   Our very special thanks to Dr. Brett-Surman of the Smithsonian Institution's
National Museum of Natural History.
   Soundprints would also like to thank Ellen Nanney and Katie Mann of the
Smithsonian Institution for their help in the creation of this book.

SURPRISE,
STEGOSAURUS!

based on text by Dawn Bentley
Illustrated by Karen Carr

A note to the reader:
Throughout this story you will see words in **bold letters**. There is more information about these words in the glossary. The glossary is in the back of the book.

One morning, a Stegosaurus walks away from her nest to a sunny spot near the lake. She is ready to start her day.

Stegosaurus looks for something tasty on the ground. With luck, the eggs in her nest will remain safe until she returns.

She snips off a
piece of **moss**
growing nearby.
She can't chew,
so she swallows
the moss whole.

Stegosaurus searches for more food. She is not fast, but she is strong!

Stegosaurus drinks from a stream. She must be careful! Sometimes an **Allosaurus** hides nearby. Stegosaurus is not fast enough to get away from the Allosaurus.

Other dinosaurs splash in the water. Suddenly, a **Dromaeosaurus** cries out in fear. Stegosaurus knows danger is near!

It's an Allosaurus! Stegosaurus swings her tail to defend herself. She **pierces** his skin. Allosaurus is hurt and falls. Stegosaurus gets away.

Stegosaurus finds a shady spot under a tree to rest. Soon she is cooled off enough to continue her search for food.

Stegosaurus finds a patch of ferns. But a primitive **Ankylosaurus** is already eating them! Luckily, there are plenty of ferns to share.

Stegosaurus returns to her nest. While she was gone, several of the babies hatched! They don't look like Stegosaurus yet, but soon they will.

The sun sets and Stegosaurus is finally full. She looks around. All is safe. She falls asleep near her babies.

Glossary

Allosaurus: Despite its size, *Allosaurus* is thought to have been a speedy hunter, running at up to 20 miles per hour.

Ankylosaurus: *Ankylosaurus* had tough skin that was covered with bony plates, and it could swing its clubbed tail to protect itself from predators.

Dromaeosaurus: This dinosaur had very sharp teeth and six-inch claws on the inner toe of each foot.

Moss: A nonflowering plant. Moss is found in moist, shady sites.

Pierce: To make a hole in something.

ABOUT THE *STEGOSAURUS*
(STEG-o-SAW-rus)

Stegosaurus lived on earth about 200 million years ago, in a time known as the Jurassic period. It was a herbivore, which means it ate only plants.

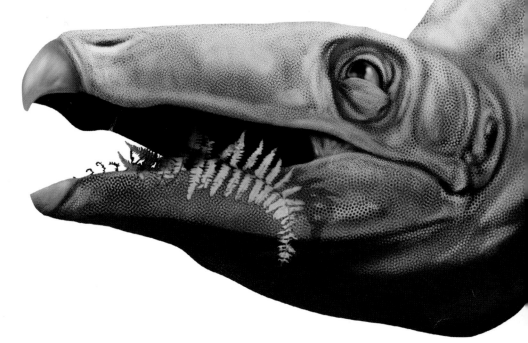

Stegosaurus weighed about two tons—that's 4,480 pounds! As you can see, *Stegosaurus* was a very big dinosaur. But its head was very small, just 18 inches long, and its brain was only about the size of a walnut. Such a tiny brain means that the *Stegosaurus* was not a very smart dinosaur.

Most paleontologists, people who study dinosaur fossils, believe that the large bony plates on the back of *Stegosaurus* were used to help control the dinosaur's body temperature. The blood near the surface of its skin would warm it up in the sun or cool it down in the shade.

Other dinosaurs that lived with Stegosaurus:

Allosaurus (AL-o-SAWR-us)

Ankylosaurus (ANG-ki-lo-SAWR-us)

Brachiosaurus (BRAK-ee-o-SAWR-us)

Dromaeosaurus (DROH-mee-o-SAWR-us)